THE LAST MAN — Safeword

THE LAST MAN — Safeword

Brian K. Vaughan
Writer

Pia Guerra
Penciller — "Safeword"

Goran Parlov
Penciller — "Widow's Pass"

José Marzán, Jr.
Inker

Zylonol
Colorist

Clem Robins
Letterer

Aron Wiesenfeld
Massimo Carnevale
Original series covers

Y: THE LAST MAN created by Brian K. Vaughan and Pia Guerra

Karen Berger
VP-Executive Editor

Will Dennis
Editor-original series

Casey Seijas
Assistant Editor-original series

Scott Nybakken
Editor-collected edition

Robbin Brosterman
Senior Art Director

Paul Levitz
President & Publisher

Georg Brewer
VP-Design & Retail Product Development

Richard Bruning
Senior VP-Creative Director

Patrick Caldon
Senior VP-Finance & Operations

Chris Caramalis
VP-Finance

Terri Cunningham
VP-Managing Editor

Stephanie Fierman
Senior VP-Sales & Marketing

Alison Gill
VP-Manufacturing

Rich Johnson
VP-Book Trade Sales

Hank Kanalz
VP-General Manager, WildStorm

Lillian Laserson
Senior VP & General Counsel

Jim Lee
Editorial Director-WildStorm

Paula Lowitt
Senior VP-Business & Legal Affairs

David McKillips
VP-Advertising & Custom Publishing

John Nee
VP-Business Development

Gregory Noveck
Senior VP-Creative Affairs

Cheryl Rubin
Senior VP-Brand Management

Bob Wayne
VP-Sales

Y: THE LAST MAN — SAFEWORD
Published by DC Comics. Cover and compilation
Copyright © 2004 DC Comics. All Rights Reserved.

Originally published in single magazine form as Y: THE LAST MAN 18-23.
Copyright © 2004 Brian K. Vaughan and Pia Guerra. All Rights Reserved.
All characters, the distinctive likenesses and related elements featured
in this publication are trademarks of Brian K. Vaughan and Pia Guerra.
VERTIGO is a trademark of DC Comics. The stories, characters and
incidents featured in this publication are entirely fictional. DC Comics
does not read or accept unsolicited submissions of ideas, stories or artwork.

DC Comics, 1700 Broadway, New York, NY 10019
A Warner Bros. Entertainment Company.
Printed in the USA. Fifth Printing.
ISBN: 978-1-4012-0232-3
Cover illustration by Aron Wiesenfeld.
Logo design by Terry Marks.

Cleveland, Ohio
Fifteen Years Ago

YOU KNOW HE GETS CONFUSED IF WE ALL TRY TO TALK WITH HIM AT THE SAME--

I DON'T CARE!

I...I DON'T EVEN *LIKE* HIM! HE ALWAYS TRIES TO TOUCH MY--

IT'S OKAY, DAD. I CAN GO IN FIRST.

THERE'S A BRAVE SOLDIER.

HE DIDN'T EVEN NEED A ST. CRISPIN'S DAY SPEECH TO GET *HIM* INTO THE FRONT LINE.

I HOPE YOU BOTH GET *AIDS*.

EXIT

HELLO?

GRAMPY...?

7

IT'S ME. YORICK.

YORICK *WHO?*

HA HA, HILARIOUS.

COME HERE, YA LITTLE BASTARD. WHAT BRINGS YOU TO THIS DUMP?

MOM'S IN TOWN FOR CAMPAIGN STUFF, REMEMBER?

HEY, HOW COME THERE ARE SO MANY WOMEN IN HERE?

WHY?

'CAUSE WOMEN LIVE LONGER THAN MEN.

'CAUSE THEY SUCK ALL THE GODDAMN *LIFE* OUT OF US.

OH.

WELL, IT MUST BE COOL TO BE, LIKE, THE ONLY GUY WITH SO MANY GIRLS ALL OVER THE PLACE.

YOU *CRAZY?* IT'S HELL ON EARTH! AIN'T *NOTHING* WORSE THAN LADIES IN NUMBERS.

SOMEDAY, YOU'LL UNDERSTAND...

Allenspark, Colorado
Now

SPAK

DOC!

I'LL TAKE CARE OF HER! GO! HIDE IN THE WOODS.

BUT AMPERSAND--

I'VE GOT HIM, JUST *RUN* ALREADY!

DR. MANN?

ALLISON? ARE YOU...?

I'M...I'M ALL RIGHT, 355.

I TOLD YOU THESE DORKY THINGS SAVE...

...LIVES?

TELL US WHERE THE THIRD GAL IN YOUR LITTLE RAIDING PARTY WENT OFF TO...OR WE START SHOOTING MORE THAN TIRES.

I THINK YOUR EYES WERE PLAYING TRICKS ON YOU, SHERIFF. THERE ARE ONLY TWO OF US, AND WE **AREN'T** HERE TO STEAL YOUR CATTLE.

WE'RE TRYING TO REACH ST. JOSEPH'S HOSPITAL IN DENVER SO WE CAN GET SOME ANTIBIOTICS FOR OUR **PET.**

HE, UH, **SHE** GOT A BAD CUT ON HER ARM A FEW DAYS BACK, AND I'M PRETTY SURE IT'S **INFECTED.** BUT IF WE HAD KNOWN THIS WAS PRIVATE PROPERTY--

AIN'T NOTHING PRIVATE ABOUT IT. LAND BARONS WENT EXTINCT SAME TIME ALL THE FELLAS DID. THIS EARTH BELONGS TO ANY WOMAN WANTS TO SET FOOT ON IT.

ANY WOMAN 'CEPT **AMAZONS,** THAT IS.

AMAZONS?

I'M AFRAID YOU'RE CONFUSED. I'M ACTUALLY--

UHN!

THAT WAS... **UNNECESSARY.**

13

I WAS SIMPLY REACHING FOR IDENTIFICATION. I'M A **FEDERAL AGENT.**

FEDERAL AGENT OF **WHAT?**

TECHNICALLY, MY ORGANIZATION IS CLASSIFIED, BUT THE PRESIDENT HAS AUTHORIZED ME TO--

SAVE THAT BULLSHIT FOR THE MAGISTRATES.

YEAH, WE BEEN WARNED ABOUT YOUR KIND...MUTILATIN' YOUR OWN TEATS, TEARING AROUND ON MOTORCYCLES, STEALING FOOD FROM DEFENSELESS WOMEN.

YOU PEOPLE HAVE NO **CLUE** WHAT YOU'RE TALKING ABOUT.

WE'RE **NOT** DAUGHTERS OF THE AMAZON!

PROVE IT.

SHOW US YOUR BREASTS.

WHAT?

RELAX, WE'RE NOT HOMOSEXUALS.

BESIDES, IF YOU'RE TELLING THE TRUTH, YOU AIN'T GOT NOTHING WE HAVEN'T ALL SEEN--

REACH FOR THE SKY, PARDNERS!

WHAT DO I CARE?

WE BREASTLESS AMAZONS *ACHE* FOR THE SWEET EMBRACE OF MOTHER OBLIVION.

SAY *WHAT?*

GIRL AIN'T RIGHT IN THE HEAD.

BUTTERCUP!

LAST CHANCE, HAND OVER YOUR WEAPONS TO MY ASSOCIATES.

THREE... *TWO...*

ALL RIGHT, ALL RIGHT!

JUST... JUST TAKE HER EASY.

BITCH.

NOW THEN.

YOU'VE GOT ABOUT A TWO-HOUR WALK BACK TO CIVILIZATION.

I'LL LEAVE YOUR WEAPONS WITH THE FIRST REPUTABLE TRADING POST WE PASS.

YOU MEAN... YOU WOMEN *AIN'T* AMAZONS?

DO *THESE* LOOK MUTILATED TO YOU, YOU IGNORANT *SHITHEADS?*

JEEZ.

SO MUCH FOR PROTECTING A LADY'S *DIGNITY...*

17

OROOOOOO

FUCK, I THINK AMPERSAND'S GETTING WORSE, 355. ARE WE ALMOST THERE?

YOU'RE NOT GOING TO THE HOSPITAL, YORICK. NOT AFTER THAT CRAP YOU PULLED BACK THERE.

WHAT? I SAVE YOUR LIVES, AND YOU PUNISH MY *MONKEY*? HE'S GONNA *DIE* WITHOUT MEDICINE!

YOU DIDN'T SAVE OUR LIVES, YOU NEEDLESSLY RISKED YOUR OWN... *AGAIN.*

ANYWAY, DR. MANN AND I ARE STILL TAKING AMPERSAND TO ST. JOSEPH'S. WE'RE JUST NOT BRINGING *YOU* WITH US.

IF THAT PONY EXPRESS CHICK WE MET IN NEBRASKA WAS TELLING THE TRUTH, ST. JOE'S IS GUARDED LIKE AREA 51.

GETTING MY HANDS ON MORE AUGMENTIN IS GOING TO TAKE PATIENCE, DIPLOMACY AND FINESSE.

QUALITIES YOU'VE NEVER EVEN *HEARD* OF.

SO YOU'RE... YOU'RE JUST GOING TO *LEAVE* ME?

NOT BY YOURSELF.

I DIDN'T WANT TO DO THIS, BUT I HAVE A COLLEAGUE WHO LIVES A FEW MILES FROM HERE.

A CULPER RING AGENT?

EX-CULPER.

SHE TOOK A PERMANENT LEAVE OF ABSENCE AFTER HER HUSBAND-SLASH-PARTNER WAS ASSASSINATED BY *17 NOVEMBER*.

WAIT, I DON'T WANT TO STAY WITH SOME SHELL-SHOCKED *WIDOW!* PLEASE! I PROMISE, I'LL BE ON MY BEST BEHAVIOR! I--

YORICK, I'VE KNOWN THIS WOMAN SINCE SHE WAS *NINE*. WE WERE IN THE SAME ORPHANAGE WHEN WE WERE BOTH RECRUITED.

AGENT 711 HAS SAVED MY ASS ALMOST AS OFTEN AS I'VE SAVED HERS. YOU'LL BE FINE.

HOLD ON, HER CODENAME IS SERIOUSLY *711?* MAN, HOW MANY GUYS USED TO ASK IF SHE'S "OPEN ALL NIGHT"?

711 WAS *GENERAL WASHINGTON'S* CODENAME DURING THE REVOLUTIONARY WAR. THAT DESIGNATION WAS AWARDED TO MY FRIEND AFTER SHE HELPED SAVE THE WORLD FROM NUCLEAR ANNIHILATION.

IF YOU MAKE A SINGLE CRACK AT HER EXPENSE, I WILL RIP OFF YOUR PENIS WITH A CLAW HAMMER.

SADDLE UP.

OH MY GOD. *355?*

LONG TIME, 711.

1033?

HE'S DEAD. 241 AND 853, TOO. *ALL* OF THE PRIMES, OBVIOUSLY.

I CAN'T IMAGINE, 355. I'M STILL NOT OVER 1451.

WE LIVE IN PROFOUNDLY STRANGE TIMES.

YEP.

711, THESE ARE MY NEW CHARGES.

MY FRIENDS.

DR. ALLISON MANN, BIOENGINEER OUT OF BOSTON. IF ANYONE CAN FIGURE OUT WHAT CAUSED THE PLAGUE, IT'S HER.

PLEASURE.

MN.

AND THIS, AS FAR AS WE KNOW, IS THE LAST MAN ON EARTH.

HIYA.

IS...IS THIS SOME KIND OF JOKE?

THAT'S WHAT I KEEP ASKING MYSELF.

HOW?

DOES...DOES THIS HAVE SOMETHING TO DO WITH THE AMULET OF HELENE?

AH, ACTUALLY, MAYBE WE SHOULD SPEAK IN PRIVATE, 711...

ALL RIGHT, DOCTOR, I THINK WE'RE READY TO RIDE.

711 HAS KINDLY OFFERED TO LOOK AFTER YORICK UNTIL WE RETURN.

COME BACK WITH A HEALTHY MONKEY, OR DON'T COME BACK AT ALL.

LIKE YOU COULD LIVE WITHOUT *ME*.

BE GOOD, 'RICK.

I'VE LEFT MY JOURNALS WITH 711, JUST SO SHE KNOWS WHAT SHE'LL BE DEALING WITH.

YOU...YOU KEEP A *JOURNAL*?

WHY DON'T YOU COME INSIDE, MR. BROWN?

I HAVE SOMETHING YOU MIGHT LIKE TO SEE.

23

HOLY CRAP!

IT'S PARADISE CITY!

THEY BELONGED TO MY HUSBAND. YOU'RE WELCOME TO BORROW AS MANY AS YOU LIKE.

YOU ARE A *GODDESS*. WHEN I LEFT BROOKLYN, ALL I TOOK WITH ME WAS A COPY OF *ZEN AND THE ART OF MOTORCYCLE MAINTENANCE*. IT'S MY GIRLFRIEND BETH'S FAVORITE BOOK, BUT I HAVE A SHORT ATTENTION SPAN FOR--

HEY, *THE DAY OF THE LOCUST*.

THIS IS THE GREATEST NOVEL OF ALL TIME!

IS THAT NATHANIEL WEST? NEVER READ HIM. I'VE ALWAYS PREFERRED *POETRY* TO PROSE.

OH, IT'S GOT THE MOST HILARIOUS CHARACTER EVER, THIS GUY NAMED *HOMER SIMPSON*.

AND THIS WAS WRITTEN ABOUT FIFTY YEARS BEFORE THE CARTOON, MIND YOU.

HOMER'S THIS AWKWARD, NAÏVE SHUT-IN WHO'S UNCOMFORTABLE WITH HIS OWN SEXUALITY, BUT HE LEAVES HIS LIFE OF SOLITUDE TO GO TO CALIFORNIA.

AND WHAT DOES HE HOPE TO FIND THERE, YORICK?

Yorick, you need to wake up.

Where the Hell Am I?

WHY ARE WE--

ISN'T IT OBVIOUS?

YEAH, USE YOUR *BRAIN*.

BUT IF *WE'RE...*?

THAT MEANS THE *WIZARD--*

GRRRRRR

AHH!

IT'S JUST THE COWARDLY LION, YORICK.

YOU *KNEW* THIS WAS COMING, DIDN'T YOU? REMEMBER WHAT THAT GIRL SAID? BEFORE SHE *DIED*?

NNN...NO... ST'AWAY...YOU CAN'T COME TO OZ...

FORGET ABOUT OZ, YORICK.

YOU'RE NOT THE LION...

THAT WAS SOMEBODY ELSE...

YOU'RE HALLUCINATING, YORICK. IT'S JUST A SIDE EFFECT OF THE *MEDICINE* I GAVE YOU.

I...I WAS WEARING A DRESS.

I BET YOU WERE...YOU LITTLE *FAGGOT.*

HEY, WHO THE HELL ARE--

OH. YEAH. NOW I 'MEMBER.

YOU'RE AGENT 24/7, RIGHT? WELL, WHEN...WHEN 355 GETS BACK HERE, SHE'S GOING TO BEAT YOU LIKE A--

IT'S AGENT 711, YORICK. AND I'VE ALREADY MOVED YOU TO A SECURE LOCATION, FAR AWAY FROM MY CABIN. I PROMISE YOU, *NO* ONE IS GOING TO FIND US.

I DON'T GET IT.

YOU AND THREE-FIFTY ARE SUPPOSED TO BE PART OF THE SAME STUPID CLUB.

WE ARE. BUT THE SUM TOTAL OF WHAT AGENT 355 DOESN'T KNOW ABOUT THE *TRUE* CULPER RING COULD JUST ABOUT FILL THE *MARIANAS TRENCH*.

THAT WOMAN HAS NO IDEA WHO WE *REALLY* ARE.

GAH!

WHAT ARE YOU SCREAMING ABOUT NOW, *FAG?*

WHY...WHY DO YOU KEEP CALLING ME THAT? I'M *STRAIGHT.*

BULLSHIT. I READ 355'S JOURNALS. YOU'VE BEEN THE ONLY MAN ON EARTH FOR *MONTHS*, AND YOU HAVEN'T HAD SEX WITH *ONE* GIRL YET.

YOU HAVEN'T EVEN *SEEN* PUSSY!

SO...TELL ME ABOUT THE FIRST TIME YOU FUCKED ANOTHER BOY.

I TOLD YOU, I'M **NOT** GAY.

NOT THAT THERE'S ANY-THING **WRONG** WITH--

AHN!

THWAP

TELL ME ABOUT YOUR FIRST GAY EXPERIENCE...OR I BRING OUT THE STRAP-ON, AND YOU CAN HAVE **ANOTHER.**

IT WASN'T LIKE THAT...

YOU HAPPY, ASSHOLE? YOU THINK YOU DISCOVERED MY ROSEBUD OR SOMETHING?

IT WAS SICK KID BULLSHIT. I TOLD MY PARENTS. I SAW A FUCKING SHRINK. IT WAS NOTHING. IT'S NOT MY SECRET ORIGIN.

METHINKS SHE DOTH PROTEST...

IS THAT WHY YOU BECAME AN ESCAPE ARTIST?

SO YOU COULD GET FREE IF SOMETHING LIKE THAT EVER HAPPENED AGAIN?

OR IS IT BECAUSE YOU LIKE REMEMBERING THE WAY IT *FELT*?

YOU WANT TO KNOW THE TRUTH...?

YOUR HIPS ARE *HUGE*, YOU FUCKING COW.

FINE.

IF THAT'S HOW WE'RE GOING TO DO THINGS...

WAIT, WHAT'S THAT?

WHAT ARE YOU--

GHHHH!

NOW. WHY DON'T YOU TELL ME ABOUT YOUR FIRST TIME...WITH A MEMBER OF THE *OPPOSITE* SEX, THAT IS.

NO! THAT'S *MINE!*

YOU CAN'T HAVE THAT! YOU... YOU...

...beth...

I WAS A SOPHOMORE AND A VIRGIN BUT SHE WAS JUST A SOPHOMORE AND WE'D BEEN FRIENDS SINCE ORIENTATION BUT STARTED HOOKING UP WITH EACH OTHER AFTER

SHE GOT DUMPED BY ONE OF MY ROOMMATES AND WE PROMISED NOT TO FALL IN LOVE BUT THEN WE DID BY ACCIDENT AND SHE MOVED OUT OF THE DORMS ON

PURPOSE AND GOT HER OWN SHITTY STUDIO APARTMENT N THE EAST VILLAGE BETWEEN A SUSHI RESTAURANT AND A PIZZA JOINT AND I SAID SHE WAS COMPLETING THE

AXIS BECAUSE SHE'S GERMAN AND WE WERE GONNA WAIT UNTIL SHE WAS ON THE PILL BUT THEN SHE GAVE ME THIS *LOOK* THAT BURNED INTO MY MIND AND THEN

The next morning, I saw the most horrifying thing I've ever seen.

I woke up before Beth, and noticed something on her floor. It was the tissues I had tossed aside just before we collapsed. They had turned **black**...

...black with **flies.**

There were dozens of them, feasting on my lust, my depravity...

...my **weakness.**

41

AND NOW THEY HAD A *TASTE* FOR IT.

FOR MONTHS, I HAD THESE NIGHTMARES ABOUT MAGGOTS CRAWLING UP MY URETHRA AND...AND NESTING IN MY *TESTICLES*.

JESUS, YOU HAVE *PROBLEMS.*

MORE ALL THE TIME...

YORICK, DO YOU EVEN *LIKE* SEX?

OF...OF COURSE.

BUT YOU THINK IT'S *FILTHY?*

I DON'T KNOW. YES. NO.

ARE YOU ATTRACTED TO ME, YORICK?

I GUESS.

A LITTLE?

A...A LOT.

THEN WHY DON'T YOU HAVE SEX WITH *ME?*

BECAUSE...

SO, UH, MOMMY SAID THAT YOU AND I SHOULD HAVE A TALK ABOUT...YOU KNOW.

I FIGURED OUT WHAT YOU'RE DOING WITH MY TRACING PAPER, YORICK! YOU'RE DRAWING PICTURES OF GIRLS WITH NO CLOTHES ON! YOU LEFT AN IMPRINT ON MY PAD, ASS!

HERO SKETCHEZ

WELL, WE CALL THEM MORTAL SINS BECAUSE THEY DEPRIVE US OF GOD'S SANCTIFYING GRACE, THUS KILLING THE SOUL.

...BECAUSE I HAVE A GIRL-FRIEND.

YOU KNOW THAT'S NOT THE *REAL* REASON, YORICK.

THIS BETH GIRL IS ON THE OTHER SIDE OF THE *WORLD*. YOU'LL NEVER FIND HER.

YOU'RE WRONG.

SO WHAT IF I AM?

WHAT DOES *SHE* HAVE TO DO WITH *US*?

I *LOVE* HER.

YOU THINK JFK DIDN'T LOVE JACKIE? YOU THINK MLK DIDN'T LOVE CORETTA?

GREAT MEN FUCK AROUND ON THEIR WOMEN, YORICK, AND WHETHER YOU LIKE IT OR NOT, YOU'RE THE *GREATEST* MAN ALIVE NOW.

I CAN'T HAVE SEX WITH YOU.

YOU CAN'T OR YOU WON'T?

BECAUSE *CAN'T* IS A PROBLEM WE CAN DEAL WITH.

GOD, ENOUGH WITH THE FUCKING JOKES ALREADY! YOU'RE A FUCKING CHILD!

I'M NOT THE ONE PLAYING DRESS-UP.

AND I'M NOT THE ONE LIVING IN DENIAL!

I MEAN, A FEW MINUTES AGO, YOU ACTUALLY SAID THE MOST HORRIFYING THING YOU'VE EVER SEEN WAS A BUNCH OF INSECTS EATING YOUR SEED!

YORICK, YOU SURVIVED A PLAGUE THAT WIPED OUT NEARLY THREE BILLION PEOPLE!

THREE! BILLION!

DO YOU HONESTLY EXPECT ME TO BELIEVE THE WORST THING YOU'VE EVER SEEN IS A FEW BUGS?

FUCK YOU.

BY ALL MEANS.

GET OFF.

I'M TRYING.

I'M SERIOUS, DON'T!

YORICK, COME ON! THIS IS YOUR *DUTY.* YOUR SPERM IS MANKIND'S LAST HOPE.

NO! DR. MANN--

--IS A *QUACK!* BILLIONS OF MEN HAD *CENTURIES* TO MAKE A CLONE AND COULDN'T. WHAT MAKES YOU THINK ONE WOMAN WILL BE ABLE TO PULL IT OFF IN A FEW *YEARS?*

FACE IT, YOU'RE ALL THAT WE HAVE!

BUT AMPERSAND--

WHAT, YOU WANT ME TO MATE WITH YOUR *MONKEY?*

BESIDES, 355 TOLD ME THAT THING WAS MOST LIKELY GOING TO *DIE* BEFORE THEY EVER REACHED THE HOSPITAL.

WHAT?

BUT... BUT YOU SAID YOU *WANTED* TO HAVE SEX WITH ME!

I'M AN AGENT OF THE *CULPER RING*, YORICK, NOT YOUR *WHORE*.

BUT YOU--

NO MEANS *NO*.

DON'T MAKE ME TELL YOU AGAIN.

I DON'T UNDERSTAND. YOU *KIDNAPPED* ME AND... AND TIED ME UP AND GAVE ME *VIAGRA* AND--

AND I WOULD HAVE FUCKED YOU, YORICK.

BUT WE BOTH KNOW THAT'S NOT WHAT YOU *REALLY* WANT.

I DON'T KNOW *WHAT* I WANT ANYMORE! GOD, I...I WAS ABOUT TO BETRAY MY *GIRLFRIEND* FOR YOU, 711!

WHY ARE YOU *DOING* THIS?

HWUUUUHHHH!

KOFF KOFF KOFF!

ACCORDING TO AGENT 355'S JOURNALS, IN SEPTEMBER OF 2002, YOU DELIBERATELY REVEALED YOURSELF TO A GROUP OF GUN-TOTING REPUBLICAN WIDOWS.

WHY?

THAT WAS A... A COMPLICATED SITUATION. YOU DON'T--

GWUH!

STOP IT!

A FEW DAYS LATER, YOU CONFRONTED A PACK OF AMAZONS, SAYING SOMETHING TO THE EFFECT OF, "IF THIS IS YOUR WORLD, I WANT OUT. JUST GO AHEAD AND KILL ME ALREADY."

THAT'S... THAT'S TAKEN OUT OF CONTEXT.

HAVE IT YOUR WAY.

HAAAAAAA!

STOP... *PLEASE*...

WEEKS LATER, YOU UNNECESSARILY INVOLVED YOURSELF IN AN ALTERCATION WITH TWO ARMED VAGRANTS ON A TRAIN FROM--

SO *WHAT?*

CHRIST, HOW MANY OF MY GODDAMN GREATEST HITS DO WE HAVE TO GO OVER? WHAT'S THE *POINT?*

HAVE YOU EVER CONTEMPLATED TAKING YOUR OWN LIFE, YORICK?

BACK INTO THE DRINK THEN...

WAIT!

JUST WAIT.

THE PLAGUE WAS 7/17, RIGHT?

THIS... THIS WAS THREE DAYS LATER. JULY TWENTIETH...

I HAD ONLY LEFT MY CRAPPY STUDIO APARTMENT ONCE SINCE THE SHIT HIT THE FAN, AND AS SOON AS I SAW WHAT WAS DOWN IN MY LOBBY, I...I WENT RIGHT BACK INSIDE.

IT'S NOT LIKE THERE WERE PLACES TO VOLUNTEER OR ANYONE TO GIVE BLOOD TO. IT WAS JUST THE END OF THE WORLD, THAT'S ALL.

YOU HAVE TO UNDERSTAND, I ONLY KNEW WHAT WAS GOING ON FROM WHAT I COULD HEAR ON THOSE LAST FEW RADIO BROADCASTS BEFORE THE BATTERIES IN MY WALKMAN RAN OUT.

I KNEW THAT ALL OF THE MEN WERE DEAD IN AT LEAST NEW YORK CITY, AND I KNEW I WOULD DIE PRETTY SOON, TOO.

I MEAN, OBVIOUSLY I WAS INFECTED WITH WHATEVER OFFED EVERYBODY ELSE, RIGHT?

WHY WOULD I BE ANY DIFFERENT?

BUT A FEW DAYS LATER, I STILL WASN'T DEAD, AND MY NEW PET AND I WERE DOWN TO TOILET WATER AND OLD CONDIMENT PACKS FOR RATIONS.

AW SEEK

SO I FINALLY DECIDED TO VENTURE OUTSIDE MY BUILDING.

WHERE WERE YOU WHEN IT HAPPENED?

'CAUSE IN NEW YORK CITY, EVERYONE THOUGHT IT WAS A SMALLPOX ATTACK OR SOMETHING, AND THE WOMEN WHO DIDN'T IMMEDIATELY FLEE THE CITY LOCKED THEMSELVES INSIDE THEIR DUCT-TAPED APARTMENT.

BROOKLYN WAS A FUCKING GHOST TOWN.

THE ONLY LOCALS LEFT WERE THE CORPSES OF GUYS WHO DIDN'T HAVE FAMILY AROUND TO RETRIEVE 'EM.

BUT SOMEWHERE AMONG ALL THOSE BODIES, I NOTICED A SINGLE DEAD *WOMAN*.

SHE WAS A POLICE OFFICER, AND MY FIRST THOUGHT WAS THAT SHE...SHE LOOKED A LITTLE LIKE MY *SISTER*.

WHAT WAS LEFT OF HER DID, ANYWAY.

APPARENTLY, SHE HAD GONE ALL HEDDA GABLER RIGHT AFTER THE PLAGUE HIT.

YOU KNOW HEDDA GABLER, RIGHT? IBSEN PLAY ABOUT A CHICK WHO SHOOTS HERSELF IN THE FACE?

BUT HEDDA SHOT HERSELF BECAUSE SHE COULDN'T ENDURE LIFE IN A PATRIARCHAL SOCIETY.

THIS COP JUST SAW THE PATRIARCHY *EVAPORATE*--SAW EVERY SEXIST PARTNER WHO EVER HIT ON HER AND EVERY SCUMMY CROOK WHO CALLED HER BITCH *DIE*-- AND SHE *STILL* KILLED HERSELF.

AND THEN I THOUGHT, IF SOME TOUGH BROAD FROM NEW YORK'S FINEST COULDN'T MAKE IT IN THIS WORLD, HOW AM *I* SUPPOSED TO?

I WAS STILL HAVING AN IMPOSSIBLE TIME COPING WITH THE TWIN TOWERS, HOW THE FUCK WAS I GONNA DEAL WITH *THIS*?

AND SUDDENLY, I FELT THIS...THIS INTENSE *JEALOUSY* FOR ALL THE OTHER GUYS AROUND ME. IT WAS LIKE, THEY HAD CROSSED THE FINISH LINE ALREADY, YOU KNOW? BUT I STILL HAD A MILLION LAPS TO RUN.

AND THEN I REMEMBERED THIS THING MY *GRANDFATHER* ONCE TOLD ME AND...

WHATEVER. I KNEW I WAS DONE.

BUT YOU WEREN'T DONE.

NOT UNLESS I'M IN HELL NOW.

YOU REALIZED THAT YOU WERE STRONGER THAN SOME PATHETIC LITTLE METER MAID.

I... I GUESS SO.

BULLSHIT!

KRACK!

AHN!

THAT WOMAN HAD THE BALLS TO DO SOMETHING YOU COULD ONLY *DREAM* OF. YOU WERE TOO MUCH OF A *COWARD* TO PULL THAT TRIGGER.

NO! AT THE LAST SECOND, I...I CHANGED MY MIND!

I GRABBED A GAS MASK FROM THE COP'S SQUAD CAR, GOT AMPERSAND, AND... AND WENT TO FIND MY *FAMILY*, TO FIND *BETH*.

IS THAT WHY YOU LEFT?

OR DEEP DOWN, DID YOU KNOW THAT IF YOU THREW YOURSELF INTO ENOUGH DANGEROUS SITUATIONS, SOONER OR LATER...

SOMEONE WOULD PUT A HOLE IN YOUR HEAD *FOR* YOU?

...DIE.

WHAT THE FUCK IS GOING ON?

THIS... THIS IS **YOUR** CABIN. YOU SAID--

I HAD TO SAY A **LOT** OF THINGS, YORICK. BUT YOU CAN RELAX NOW. IT'S OVER.

WHAT'S OVER?

WHAT THE **FUCK** IS OVER?

YOUR SUICIDE INTERVENTION.

MY **WHAT?**

IT'S CALLED *LE PRÉCEDÉ D'ENFER,* A FORM OF AVERSION THERAPY DEVELOPED DURING A SECRET MEETING BETWEEN BENJAMIN FRANKLIN AND THE MARQUIS DE SADE.

IT'S BASED ON THE IDEA THAT YOUR SEXUALITY AND MORTALITY ARE INDISSOLUBLE ELEMENTS OF--

WHAT... WHAT **ARE** YOU?

I'M AN AGENT OF THE CULPER RING. I HELP GET PEOPLE WHERE THEY NEED TO BE.

IT'S WHAT WE **DO.**

JESUS, DID...DID **355** KNOW ABOUT THIS?

IS THAT WHY SHE BROUGHT ME TO YOU?

NO, THIS WAS MY DECISION AND MY DECISION ALONE. AFTER RECOGNIZING YOUR SYMPTOMS IN 355'S JOURNALS, I FELT IT WAS NECESSARY TO TAKE DRASTIC MEASURES.

BUT IF 355 **DID** HAVE SOMETHING TO DO WITH THIS, WOULD...WOULD YOU TELL ME?

RIGHT.

BUT...HOW DID YOU **KNOW**? EVERYONE ELSE JUST THINKS I'M DUMB AND IMPULSIVE AND...WELL, NOT THAT I'M **NOT**, BUT HOW DID YOU KNOW THAT I--

LIFE IS MISERY, YORICK.

YOU'RE NOT THE ONLY ONE WHO EVER WANTED TO GET IT OVER WITH.

OH, WELL, I'M...I'M SORRY I HIT YOU AT THE END OF OUR, *um,* **SESSION.**

YORICK, I JAMMED A HYPODERMIC IN YOUR NECK AND CALLED YOU **FAGGOT.**

YOU HAVE NOTHING TO APOLOGIZE FOR.

BUT IT WAS **INCREDIBLE,** 711! THE LAST TIME I WENT UNDER, I SAW--

THE PROCESS IS BASED ON SECRECY, YORICK. ANY EPIPHANIES YOU MAY HAVE HAD DURING YOUR JOURNEY SHOULD BE KEPT TO YOURSELF.

BUT DON'T YOU WANT TO KNOW WHAT I SAW THAT...THAT MADE ME WANT TO **LIVE**?

NO.

BUT WHATEVER IT WAS, DON'T **FUCKING** FORGET IT.

355! DR. MANN!

WHERE'S AMPERSAND? IS...IS HE...?

HE'S **FINE**, YORICK.

ALTHOUGH THE ANTIBIOTICS MAKE HIS STOOL EXTREMELY SOFT, AS THE UNGRATEFUL LITTLE **FUCK** WILL BE HAPPY TO SHOW YOU.

YES!

YOU TWO FOUND A WAY INSIDE THE HOSPITAL?

EVENTUALLY, ALTHOUGH IT WAS A BIT MORE OF AN **EVENT** THAN I WOULD HAVE LIKED.

I WONDER IF ETHER-RAGGING A SECURITY GUARD IS A VIOLATION OF MY HIPPOCRATIC OATH?

HOW ABOUT YOU, YORICK? YOU DO ANYTHING **EXCITING**?

NOT UNLESS YOU CALL READING THREE HUNDRED PAGES OF *WAR AND PEACE* EXCITING.

MURN MURN

HE DIDN'T CAUSE TOO MUCH TROUBLE, DID HE?

I HARDLY KNEW HE WAS HERE.

I CAN'T THANK YOU ENOUGH FOR THIS, 711. IF YOU WANT TO JOIN US FOR THE LAST LEG OF OUR TRIP TO SAN FRAN, I COULD USE A HAND WITH MY *OTHER* ASSIGNMENT AFTER I GET 'RICK TO--

I APPRECIATE IT, SWEETIE, BUT I HAVEN'T BEEN IN THE FIELD SINCE MY HUSBAND DIED. I'D JUST GET IN THE WAY.

THIS IS WHERE I BELONG NOW.

WELL, IT WAS GOOD TO HANG, 711.

THANKS FOR THE, UH, READING MATERIAL.

I THINK YOU'LL ENJOY IT, YORICK, AS LONG AS YOU'RE PATIENT. TRY NOT TO SKIP AHEAD, OKAY?

ENDINGS HAVE TO BE *EARNED.*

OH, NOT *YOU* FUCKS.

WHAT'S WITH THE GETUPS? THOSE SUPPOSED TO BE *IRONIC?*

SOMETHING LIKE THAT.

LISTEN, WE HAVE REASON TO BELIEVE THAT THE AMULET OF HELENE MAY HAVE PASSED THROUGH HERE ALREADY.

I HAVE NO IDEA WHAT YOU'RE--

KLICK

KLICK

KLICK

FINE.

I'VE GOT IT RIGHT HERE. JUST LET ME--

DON'T!

PAFT

PAFT

PAFT

Queensbrook, Arizona
Now

YOUR DADDY WOULD BE SO PROUD OF YOU RIGHT NOW, LEAH.

YOU LOOK LIKE A MILLION DAMN DOLLARS.

AW, SHUT UP, MOM.

JOY'S RIGHT, KID.

HECK, YOU'RE ONE TUBE OF REVLON SHY OF A DEBUTANTE BALL!

ALL RIGHT, TAKE HER *EASY*, ANGELENE. I'M ALL FOR HAVING A GOOD TIME HERE, BUT LET'S NOT FORGET THAT TWO OF OUR BEST ARE IN CRITICAL TONIGHT.

'COURSE.

NO DISRESPECT.

LEAH, YOU WANNA TELL US WHY YOU'RE HERE THIS EVENING, IN THE 227TH YEAR OF THIS ONCE-GREAT NATION'S INDEPENDENCE?

UM, TO DEFEND THE LIBERTY OF THE CITIZENS OF THE STATE OF ARIZONA, THROUGH EDUCATION AND SERVICE.

YEP.

AND AS AN OFFICIAL MEMBER OF OUR BROTHERHOOD, WHO ELSE WILL YOU WELCOME TO APPLY FOR MEMBERSHIP?

ALL MEN AND WOMEN... WELL, JUST *WOMEN* NOW...OVER THE AGE OF SIXTEEN, REGARDLESS OF, UH... RACE OR CREED, SO LONG AS THEY SUPPORT OUR CONSTITUTION.

THAT'S MY DARLING.

LEAH, I WAS SAVING THIS FOR ONE OF YOUR *BROTHERS'* INDUCTIONS, BUT SINCE THEY'RE NO LONGER WITH US...

FOR SERIOUS?

YOU SWEAR TO ALWAYS DO WHAT'S RIGHT FOR YOUR BELOVED STATE?

HELL, YEAH.

EVEN IF...?

Fourteen Miles East
Six Hours Earlier

WHAT'S YOUR POISON, 355?

I DON'T KNOW. MAYBE THOSE THINGS THEY USED AT SCHOOL BEFORE PHOTOCOPIES... *MIMEOGRAPHS?*

I LIKED THE WAY THEY SMELLED WHEN THEY WERE WARM.

MIMEOGRAPHS?

WHEN WERE YOU A STUDENT, THE 1800'S?

I'M ONLY A FEW YEARS OLDER THAN *YOU*, ASSFACE.

HOW ABOUT YOU, DR. MANN?

PYGMY SHREWS.

YOU...LIKE THE SMELL OF PYGMY SHREWS?

I DON'T GIVE A FUCK ABOUT THE SMELL OF ANYTHING.

THE PYGMY SHREW JUST BECAME *EXTINCT.*

RIGHT THIS SECOND?

IT'S BEEN MORE THAN A YEAR AND A HALF SINCE THE PLAGUE KILLED EVERY MAMMAL WITH A PENIS EXCEPT FOR YOU AND AMPERSAND, CORRECT?

WELL, AS FAR AS WE--

THE PYGMY SHREW HAS A *LIFESPAN* OF A YEAR AND A HALF. WITH NOTHING LEFT TO GET KNOCKED UP BY, THAT MEANS THEY'RE GONE NOW. *ALL* OF THEM.

IN A FEW MONTHS OPOSSUMS WILL BE WIPED OUT, TOO.

HOW SERIOUS IS THAT, ALLISON?

HOW *SERIOUS?* IN THE GRAND SCHEME OF THINGS? WHO GIVES A SHIT?

BUT A FEW MONTHS AFTER THAT, THE LAST *RATS* WILL START TO DIE. AND AFTER *THEY* DIE--

DOGGIES!

YORICK, ARE YOU RETARDED? MOST CANINES LIVE--

NO, I MEAN... DOGGIES!

RRRRRR

RRRRRR

RRRRRRR

LOOKS LIKE THERE WERE ABOUT SIX OF THEM. MAYBE MORE, BUT THE BUZZARDS PROBABLY--

WHAT IS *WRONG* WITH PEOPLE?

THE HIGHWAYS ARE OPEN OUT HERE! I MEAN, IT WASN'T RUSH HOUR WHEN THE PLAGUE HIT *THIS* TIME ZONE. HOW MANY CARS HAVE DRIVEN PAST THESE GUYS SINCE THEN?

AND NOT *ONE* WOMAN CAN STOP AND... AND GIVE THEM A DECENT BURIAL?

I'M SORRY, 'RICK, BUT YOU KNOW THE STORY.

WHEN THREE BILLION PEOPLE DIE IN ONE DAY--

YO!

GET AWAY FROM THOSE BOYS!

ISN'T THIS THE PART WHERE YOU DO SOMETHING STUPID?

THAT WAS OLD YORICK.

NEW YORICK *AVOIDS* THE VIOLENT FEMMES.

WHAT ARE YOU TALKING ABOUT?

YOU CAME AT US WITH A *WEAPON*.

CAME AT YOU? I WAS OUT HUNTING *DINNER*. I HEARD A SHOT, SO I...I CAME RUNNING.

TO SAVE OUR LIVES?

YES! THE LOCAL MILITIA PSYCHOS HAVE RIGGED CORPSES WITH BOOBY TRAPS TO... TO SCARE AWAY "OUTSIDERS."

I DIDN'T WANT TO SEE SOME GOOD SAMARITAN GET HER HAND BLOWN OFF BY A CLAYMORE.

WHY SHOULD WE BELIEVE SOME SKINHEAD?

HEY, THIS IS *PRACTICAL,* NOT POLITICAL. IN CASE YOU HAVEN'T NOTICED, LONG LOCKS AND DESERT HEAT GO TOGETHER LIKE ORANGE JUICE AND COLGATE.

AND NOW THAT THE LESS-FAIR SEX HAS PASSED ON, OUR HAIR IS PRETTY MUCH...

...

IS THAT A *DUDE?*

ME? UH, NO.

SEE, I HAVE REAL BAD ALLERGIES, SO--

OKAY, THAT IS THE *WORST* FAKE CHICK VOICE I HAVE EVER HEARD. AND LOOK AT YOUR HANDS! YOU'RE *TOTALLY* A DUDE!

MY COMPANION HAS A HORMONE CONDITION THAT MAKES HER LOOK AND SOUND--

OH, GIVE IT UP, AGENT 355. JUST TELL HER THE TRUTH. WHAT *DIFFERENCE* DOES IT MAKE?

HIDIGEY, IDIGALLIDIGISIDIGON! ZIDIGIP IDIGIT!

DIDIGONT YIDIGOU *TIDIGELL* MIDIGE WHIDIGAT TIDIGO DIDIGO!

DON'T MIND THEM. THEY DO THIS ALL THE TIME. I THINK IT'S *CHINESE.*

ALL RIGHT, NOW I *KNOW* YOU'RE A DUDE. THAT'S *GIBBERISH,* IT'S LIKE PIG LATIN ONLY GIRLS KNOW HOW TO SPEAK.

NEVER HEARD ANYBODY DO IT THAT FAST THOUGH.

OH, WHAT THE FUCK?

YOU GUYS TOLD ME THAT WAS CHINESE!

86

HOLY...

YOU...YOU *ARE* A MAN. I DIDN'T REALLY *BELIEVE*...

WHOOPSIE-DAISY.

FIDIGUCKIDIGING *HIDIGELL.*

YES, YORICK IS--IN THE LOOSEST SENSE OF THE WORD-- A *MAN.*

AND IF YOU TAKE US SOME-WHERE WHERE WE CAN SIT DOWN AND REFILL OUR CANTEENS, WE'LL TELL YOU THE WHOLE *UNBEARABLY TEDIOUS* STORY.

MY...MY GARAGE IS RIGHT UP THE ROAD.

JESUS, AM I DREAMING?

LADY, *DAVID LYNCH'S* DREAMS WEREN'T THIS WEIRD.

FRN ADK

P.J.'s GAS

Certified Welding
and other crap

WOW, YOU REALLY KNOW WHAT TO DO WITH ALL THIS STUFF, P.J.?

WELL, *THAT'S* CONDESCENDING.

BUT YEAH, I FIGURE I'M PROBABLY THE ONLY PERSON STILL ALIVE WHO CAN FIX A WASSER-BOXER PANCAKE WITH A BROKEN STEEL TIMING BELT.

I WISH WE HAD YOU AROUND WHEN OUR PIECE OF SHIT MINIVAN BROKE DOWN OUTSIDE TUBA CITY.

TELL ME ABOUT IT. I'D PROBABLY BE A MILLIONAIRE BY NOW... IF THOSE *SONS OF ARIZONA* BITCHES HADN'T CHOKED TRAFFIC DOWN TO LESS THAN ZERO.

WHO?

SONS OF ARIZONA...WHICH WAS A PRETTY STUPID NAME FOR A MILITIA EVEN WHEN ALL THE MEN *WEREN'T* DEAD. THEY'RE THE SAME CHICKS WHO RIGGED THOSE DEAD GUYS TO BLOW.

THE S.O.A. THINK THE *FEDERAL GOVERNMENT* IS RESPONSIBLE FOR THE PLAGUE, SO IN SOME KIND OF FUCKED-UP PROTEST, THEY CUT INTERSTATE 40 IN TWO.

OH, CHRIST.

THE McVEIGH GAMBIT.

THE WHAT NOW?

TIMOTHY McVEIGH, THE FUCKWAD WHO BLEW UP THE MURRAH BUILDING.

BEFORE THAT, HE WAS WORKING ON A PLAN TO SEIZE CONTROL OF A FEW HILLS AROUND I-40 IN ORDER TO SHUT DOWN THE ENTIRE INTERSTATE.

WITH THAT ONE ACT, THESE EIGHT ASSHOLES HAVE SINGLE-HANDEDLY STOPPED NINETY PERCENT OF THE GROUND SHIPMENT BETWEEN EAST AND WEST.

EIGHT?

EIGHT WOMEN ARE RESPONSIBLE FOR HALF OF THE COUNTRY *STARVING* TO DEATH?

EIGHT EXCEPTIONALLY *WELL-ARMED* WOMEN. DOZEN TEXAS RANGERS TRIED TO STORM THIER BLOCKADE ABOUT A WEEK AGO. ALL BUT *ONE* OF THEM WERE KILLED.

SURVIVOR TOLD ME THEY ONLY MANAGED TO WOUND TWO OF THE BAD GUYS BEFORE HER FRIENDS WERE COMPLETELY WIPED OUT.

IF INTERSTATE 40 IS NO LONGER AN OPTION, HOW THE HELL ARE WE GOING TO REACH MY BACKUP LAB IN SAN FRANCISCO?

SAN FRAN?

IF YOU GUYS ARE HEADED UP THERE, WHY DIDN'T YOU JUST GO THROUGH UTAH?

WE TRIED.

UNFORTUNATELY, A MASSIVE FOREST FIRE IS CURRENTLY *CONSUMING* MOST OF THAT STATE.

WITH SO FEW FEMALE FIREFIGHTERS AROUND, 355 THOUGHT IT WOULD BE SAFER TO DETOUR THROUGH ARIZONA THAN TO RISK A TRIP THROUGH MORMON HELLFIRE.

 OUT OF THE FRYING PAN, HUH?

WELL, YOU CAN ALWAYS HAVE A TRUCK FROM MY FLEET, TAKE YOUR CHANCES WITH AN ALTERNATE ROUTE.

 HOW MANY CHOICES DO WE HAVE LEFT? I-10? I-8?

WHAT IF RUBY RIDGE LUNATICS HAVE TAKEN *THOSE* ROADS HOSTAGE?

THEN WE'LL GO DOWN TO MEXICO AND COME UP THROUGH SAN DIEGO.

 BULLSHIT! WE CAN'T AFFORD TO WASTE ANY MORE TIME, 355!

WHAT DO YOU WANT ME TO DO, ALLISON? DRAG YOU AND YORICK THROUGH A *WARZONE?*

ISN'T THAT WHAT YOU'VE BEEN DOING FOR THE LAST EIGHTEEN MONTHS? BESIDES, I THOUGHT YOUR LITTLE CLUB WAS *CREATED* TO DEAL WITH CRAP LIKE THIS!

 THE REST OF THE CULPER RING AND I WILL WORK ON OPENING INTERSTATE 40...*AFTER* I GET YOU AND YORICK TO OUR FINAL DESTINATION.

WHEN WILL THAT BE, A *YEAR* FROM NOW?

BY THEN, SOME AMAZON WILL HAVE PROBABLY TORCHED *EVERYTHING* I USED TO MAKE MY DAUGHTER!

 DAUGHTER?

DOC, YOU TOLD US THAT CLONE YOU GAVE BIRTH TO WAS A *BOY.*

AND THIS ISN'T THE FIRST TIME YOU'VE SUGGESTED OTHERWISE...

WHAT, AM I BEING *INTERROGATED* NOW? IT WAS A SLIP OF THE FUCKING TONGUE.

YOU'RE THE ONE WITH ALL THE SECRETS, 355! MAYBE THIS MILITIA IS RIGHT. MAYBE YOUR BOSSES *ARE* TO BLAME FOR THIS WHOLE GODDAMN NIGHTMARE.

ALLISON...

FORGET IT.

I NEED SOME AIR.

JEEZ, *PMS* MUCH?

I DIDN'T SAY IT.

I'M SORRY ABOUT THAT... AND I'M SORRY ABOUT BEFORE, P.J. THIS TRIP HASN'T BEEN EASY ON ANY OF US.

HEY, WATER UNDER THE WHATEVER. YOU GUYS ARE STILL WELCOME TO BUNK HERE TONIGHT, FIGURE OUT YOUR NEXT MOVE TOMORROW.

IT'S LIKE MY OLD MAN USED TO SAY...

...EVERYTHING LOOKS BETTER AFTER A GOOD NIGHT'S SLEEP.

92

THEN RUN AWAY! BEFORE IT COMES!

IT CAN *SMELL* ME! IT CAN--

SNFF

XXXXXXXX

YORICK!

YORICK, GET UP!

IS DR. MANN WITH YOU?

WHA?

NO, WHY WOULD SHE--

SHE'S MISSING!

ONE MINUTE SHE WAS SLEEPING ACROSS FROM ME, AND THE NEXT SHE'S GONE.

GONE WHERE? DID SINEAD DO SOMETHING TO--

I'M RIGHT HERE, DICK.

AND I DIDN'T HEAR HER LEAVE EITHER. ALL OF MY VEHICLES ARE STILL AROUND, TOO.

WELL, THAT'S GOOD.

I MEAN, SHE PROBABLY JUST WENT FOR A MIDNIGHT STROLL OR SOMETHING... RIGHT?

Queensbrook, Arizona
Now

WELL, *THAT'S* GOING TO END BADLY.

COME ON, THIS IS IMPORTANT.

I TOLD YOU, 355, I HAVE NO IDEA *WHERE* DR. MANN WENT!

I KNOW, BUT I'M AFRAID I DO.

WHAT DOES *THAT* MEAN?

IT MEANS I HAVE TO GO AFTER HER, BEFORE SHE DOES SOMETHING SHE'LL REGRET.

YOU'RE *LEAVING?* BUT THE LAST TIME YOU PAWNED ME OFF TO SOME WOMAN, IT WAS... *STRANGE.*

AND THAT WAS ONE OF YOUR *FRIENDS!* WE'VE ONLY KNOWN KOJACK BACK THERE FOR A FEW HOURS!

'RICK, IF P.J. WANTED TO HURT YOU, SHE WOULD HAVE DONE IT ALREADY.

BUT JUST IN CASE, I'M LEAVING YOU WITH *THIS.*

MY NAME IS ALLISON MANN. I'M A *DOCTOR.*

WELL, THAT ACCENT ISN'T LOCAL.

NO, I'M FROM... ALL OVER, REALLY.

YOU AN ABORTIONIST?

SAVE IT, ANGELENE. LEAH, CHECK HER OUT?

SURE THING, MOM.

I'M JOY. WHAT BUSINESS YOU GOT WITH THE *SONS OF ARIZONA,* DOCTOR?

TWO OF MY FRIENDS AND I ARE TRYING TO GET TO CALIFORNIA.

IT'S A MEDICAL EMERGENCY, SO I WAS HOPING YOU PEOPLE WOULD BE KIND ENOUGH TO LET US THROUGH YOUR... *OBSTRUCTION.*

SORRY, BILLY GOAT GRUFF. *NOBODY* CROSSES FOR FREE.

ACTUALLY, I WAS HOPING I COULD **BARTER** FOR OUR SAFE PASSAGE.

DOC, THIS IS A POLITICAL REVOLUTION, NOT A **TOLLBOOTH.**

BESIDES, BEHIND ME IS THE MOST WELL-STOCKED COMPOUND IN THE **HEMISPHERE.** WHAT COULD **YOU** POSSIBLY HAVE THAT WE MIGHT NEED?

THE MECHANIC UP THE ROAD SAID THAT TWO OF YOUR GIRLS WERE RECENTLY **WOUNDED** IN A FIREFIGHT.

I'D LIKE TO OFFER THEM MY MEDICAL EXPERTISE.

WOMAN, THE "GIRLS" YOU'RE REFERRING TO WERE SOLDIERS OF VALOR. AND I SAY "WERE" BECAUSE BOTH OF THEM **PASSED ON** LAST NIGHT.

I'M...VERY SORRY. I WISH I HAD MADE IT HERE SOONER.

AND WHAT THE HELL DIFFERENCE WOULD THAT'VE MADE?

WHAT DID YOU THINK? THAT EVERYONE OUT HERE IS SOME BACK-WARDS HICK? THAT WE DON'T KNOW HOW TO DRESS A **GSW?** GIVE A BLOOD TRANSFUSION?

I WAS A NURSE MANAGER IN AN **ER** FOR NINE **DAMN** YEARS, YOU CONDESCENDING PIECE OF **SHIT!**

I DIDN'T MEAN--

KRACK

SEE THAT, DARLING? KNOCKING SOMEONE OUT--EVEN A CIVVIE--ISN'T NEARLY AS SIMPLE AS IT LOOKS ON THE TV.

AHHHHHN!

DEFINITELY.

KRACK

WHY DOESN'T SHE JUST PLAY POSSUM?

SURVIVAL INSTINCT'S A BITCH THAT WAY. BRAIN WANTS YOUR BODY TO STAY UP, KEEP FIGHTIN' LONG AS IT CAN.

FUHH

HERE. YOU GIVE HER A TRY.

KRACK

ANYWAY, WHAT'S UP FOR YOU AFTER CALI?

IF 355 WILL LET ME, I'D LIKE TO GO TO AUSTRALIA, FIND MY GIRLFRIEND BETH.

AWW, THAT'S ROMANTIC... AND KIND OF STUPID.

IT'S THE DUAL NATURE OF MY CHARM.

HOW ABOUT YOU, P.J.? YOU CAN'T STAY IN MILITIA-VILLE FOREVER.

BULLSHIT! I'M NOT GONNA LET SOME SKANKS WHO'VE SEEN RED DAWN ONE TIME TOO MANY SCARE ME OFF. I WAS BORN AND RAISED HERE, AND THIS IS WHERE I'M GONNA KICK.

YOU WERE RAISED IN A GARAGE?

UP UNTIL I WAS SIXTEEN. THEN MY OLD MAN WANTED ME TO START WORKING FOR HIM, SO I RAN AWAY TO L.A., JOINED A CRAPPY SKA BAND.

I NEVER KNEW HOW MUCH I FUCKING LOVED CARS UNTIL I WAS SURROUNDED BY PEOPLE WHO DIDN'T KNOW JACK ABOUT 'EM.

EVERYONE WAS WAY MORE IMPRESSED THAT I COULD CHANGE THEIR OIL THAN THE FACT THAT I COULD HALF-WAY PLAY BASS...SO I CAME BACK.

I USED TO THINK DAD WAS TRYING TO KEEP ME DOWN BY MAKING ME GET INTO THE FAMILY BUSINESS, BUT I REALIZE IT WAS SORTA EMPOWERING, YOU KNOW?

A GUY TEACHING HIS ONLY DAUGHTER TO BE A GREASE MONKEY? FUCK, I HOPE I'M THAT BADASS WHEN I HAVE KIDS.

YOU... WANT TO HAVE CHILDREN?

NOT WITH *YOU*, SPAZ.

THEN... *HOW?*

I DON'T KNOW. IF YOU AND YOUR FRIENDS DON'T FIND A WAY, *SOMEBODY* WILL.

IT'S NOT LIKE WE'RE JUST GONNA BECOME *EXTINCT.*

SAID THE T-REX TO THE TRICERATOPS.

DINOSAURS DIDN'T REALLY *DIE,* YORICK. THEY JUST EVOLVED INTO SOMETHING NEW.

THAT'S PROBABLY WHAT'LL HAPPEN TO WOMEN. WE'LL ALL TURN INTO *BIRDS* OR WHATEVER.

WELL, YOUR OPTIMISM IS REFRESHING... AND KIND OF *STUPID.*

TO BIRDS OF A FEATHER THEN.

FROM MY PRIVATE STOCK. THEY'RE HOTTER THAN HELL SINCE I SAVE MY GENERATORS FOR THE *LIGHTS,* BUT I DON'T THINK THEY'VE SKUNKED YET.

OH, NO THANKS, P.J. I HAVE THE TOLERANCE OF A THIRD-GRADER. AND THE LAST TIME I GOT DRUNK, I STARTED SINGING IN *SPANISH* AND--

COME ON, STRAIGHT EDGE.

HOW BAD CAN *ONE* BREW BE?

WHAT'S THE SITUATION IN THERE, MOM?

I'M LETTING ANGELENE PLAY BAD COP FOR A SPELL.

THAT DOCTOR'S HIDING SOMETHING, ALL RIGHT. I JUST CAN'T TELL *WHAT*.

YOU THINK TEXAS SENT HER? AS A SCOUT FOR MORE RANGERS OR SOMETHING?

EITHER THAT, OR THE SHADOW GOVERNMENT IS FINALLY MOVING INTO *PHASE TWO*.

I FIGURED IT WOULD TAKE ABOUT THIS LONG FOR CONDIE TO GET HER STORMTROOPERS OUT HERE.

LEAH, WHY DON'T YOU TAKE MY FORTY-SEVEN AND RUN SOME RECON ON P.J.'S?

I'VE LET THAT HAIRLESS DESERT RAT HOLD HER GROUND 'CAUSE HER DADDY WAS OKAY PEOPLE, BUT IF SHE'S HARBORING *FEDS*, OUR TRUCE IS OVER.

MAN, I WAS HOPING I COULD HELP INTERROGATE THE P.O.W.

DON'T WORRY, BABY.

IT'S NOT LIKE SHE'S *GOING* ANY-WHERE...

IF YOU DON'T WANNA GET SMACKED AGAIN, JUST ANSWER THE QUESTION.

HOW DID YOU KILL ALL THE MEN?

WAS IT A SATELLITE OR THE MEASLES VACCINATIONS? OR THOSE LITTLE ROBOTS IN THE BLOOD... *NANITES*, RIGHT?

JOY THINKS MAYBE THE U.N. HID SOMETHING IN ALL THE *PORNO*, BUT I KNOW THAT AIN'T IT. MY ERNIE NEVER WATCHED A'ONE OF THOSE IN HIS FORTY YEARS.

FUNNY SEEING YOU HERE.

SAY WHAT?

HKK

YOU GET THAT OUT OF MY KIT?

YEP.

SMART.

ONE OF US HAS TO BE.

YOU OKAY?

BEEN BETTER. YOU SHOULDN'T HAVE COME 355.

NO KIDDING. I HAD TO CRAWL THROUGH A GODDAMN MAKESHIFT *SEWAGE SYSTEM* BEFORE SNEAKING PAST A HALF-DOZEN HEAVILY ARMED--

THAT'S NOT WHAT I MEANT.

I DON'T DESERVE YOUR HELP.

I *LIED* TO YOU.

DOCTOR, CAN WE MAYBE SAVE THE DRAMATIC CONFESSIONS UNTIL WE'RE OUT OF THE KILL ZONE?

I DIDN'T BRING THE *BOY* ALONG, SO THESE CUFFS ARE GOING TO TAKE SOME--

355, BACK IN BOSTON, I LIED TO YOU ABOUT MY *BABY*.

I TOLD YOU THAT I'D CLONED MY *NEPHEW* BECAUSE WE COULDN'T FIND A TRANSPLANT DOCTOR OR SOME BULLSHIT...BUT I DON'T EVEN *HAVE* A NEPHEW. THAT WAS JUST A SOB STORY I *MADE UP*.

WHY?

I WAS SCARED. I...I THOUGHT THE GOVERNMENT HAD SENT YOU TO *ARREST* ME. I FIGURED YOU'D SHOW SOME MERCY IF MY EXPERIMENTS SOUNDED ALTRUISTIC.

SO WAIT, YOU *NEVER* GAVE BIRTH TO A CLONE?

OH, I DID...BUT IT WASN'T A BOY. IT WAS *ME*. I WAS PREGNANT WITH A CLONE OF *MYSELF*.

AT LEAST, THAT'S WHAT SHE WAS *SUPPOSED* TO BE. WHAT CAME OUT OF MY WOMB...IT WAS JUST A MESS OF LIMBS...AND *ORGANS* AND--

ALLISON...

NO, YOU DON'T UNDERSTAND. HER CONCEPTION WAS TOTALLY SELFISH AND...AND *IRRESPONSIBLE*.

BACK IN JAPAN, MY ASSHOLE FATHER WAS CLOSE TO CLONING *HIMSELF*, AND I WANTED TO SUCCEED BEFORE HE DID. WHO EVEN KNOWS IF HE EVER--

DOCTOR, WITH ALL DUE RESPECT, WHAT DOES THE SEX OF YOUR DEAD CHILD MATTER *NOW*?

DON'T YOU *GET* IT?

IT MATTERS BECAUSE IT MEANS I'M A FUCKING *FAILURE!*

COMPARED TO A BIOENGINEER LIKE MY DAD, I'M SLOW AND...AND *INCOMPETENT*. THE PLAGUE DIDN'T KILL MY BABY, MY SHODDY SCIENCE DID!

EVEN IF I *DO* FIGURE OUT WHAT CAUSED ALL THE MEN TO DIE, IT MIGHT TAKE ME *YEARS* TO SUCCESSFULLY CLONE A HUMAN BEING! YEARS THE WORLD DOESN'T HAVE!

YOU'RE IN *SHOCK*, DOCTOR. JUST TRY TO--

WE DON'T HAVE TIME, 355! WE DON'T HAVE TIME FOR MORE DETOURS AND...AND *SIDE TRIPS!* IT'S IMPERATIVE THAT I GET TO MY LAB AND START WORKING *NOW*.

THAT'S WHY I RISKED MY *LIFE* TO CUT THROUGH THIS--

ANGELENE?

...WHO THE HOLY HELL ARE *YOU*?

IF YOU MAKE ANOTHER SOUND, I WILL EMPTY THIS CLIP THROUGH YOUR *MOUTH*.

THAT .45 OF YOURS...IT'S *GOVERNMENT* ISSUE.

I WAS *RIGHT*.

GIVE ME THE KEYS TO HER HANDCUFFS.

NOW.

YOU LOOK GOOD WITH A GUN, FED, BUT YOU AIN'T A *KILLER*.

KLIK

OH, YOU'VE KILLED BEFORE. ANYONE CAN SEE THAT. BUT JUST 'CAUSE YOU DANCE DON'T MEAN YOU'RE A *DANCER*.

YOU FOLKS DON'T KNOW WHAT IT FEELS LIKE TO PULL A TRIGGER FOR YOUR HOME, FOR YOUR *FAMILY*. THAT'S WHY YOU'RE SO SLOW.

THAT'S WHY YOU'RE NOT GONNA SHOOT *ME*.

HELLLLP!

BITCH!

JUST LEAVE ME! TAKE YORICK AND--

SHUT UP!

THNK

WHAT THE FUCK IS--

HAA!

AND SPANKING THE MONKEY'S *ENOUGH?*

THE WAY METHADONE IS ENOUGH FOR A HEROIN ADDICT, I GUESS.

AND *PLEASE* DON'T BRING MONKEYS INTO THIS...

HOW MANY TIMES?

IN A DAY? WELL, THERE WAS ONE PARTICULARLY TRYING INCIDENT DURING THE *CHICAGO* LEG OF OUR TRIP, AFTER WE STOPPED BY THESE OUTDOOR SHOWERS THE CITY HAD SET UP.

BY THE TIME I WAS DONE WITH THAT NIGHT'S SESSION, I WAS SO SPENT I THINK *BONE MARROW* STARTED COMING OUT.

I KNOW I SOUND REPRESSED, BUT I'M NOT SURE I COULD LIVE WITH THE ALTERNATIVE. PREYING ON LONELY WOMEN'S...*DESPERATION,* YOU KNOW?

HUH. I CAN RESPECT THAT, ACTUALLY. I MEAN, NO OFFENSE, BUT YOU'RE NOT EXACTLY THE KINDA GUY I WOULDA FUCKED *BEFORE* THE PLAGUE, SO I WOULDN'T FEEL RIGHT FUCKING YOU *NOW.*

THAT WOULD SORTA DEGRADE US BOTH.

THAT IS THE NICEST THING ANYONE HAS EVER SAID TO ME.

CHEERS, BIG EARS.

DOWN THE HATCH, TIGHT--

RARF RARF RARF RARF RARF RARF

117

RARF RARF RARF RARF RARF RARF

WHAT THE HELL IS THAT ALL ABOUT?

SOUNDS LIKE THOSE WILD DOGS.

NO KIDDING, RETARD. WHY ARE THEY GOING *NUTS*?

MAYBE IT'S JUST 355 AND... AND DR. MANN COMING BACK.

AND MAYBE IT'S NOT.

P.J., DON'T!

I JUST REMEMBERED, I HAD THIS...THIS CRAZY VIVID *NIGHTMARE*. ABOUT SOMETHING *AWFUL* COMING. IF YOU GO OUT THERE--

YORICK, YOU'RE *SMASHED*. GO HIDE UNDER A DESK OR SOMETHING. I'LL BE RIGHT BACK.

BUT...

ARR FARR

I KNOW, ALL RIGHT! I'M NOT GOING TO *USE* IT, I JUST--

HEY!

YOU! WHAT THE HELL ARE-- UHN!

P.J.?

BANG

Queensbrook, Arizona
Now

OH.

OH, FUCK.

THAT...THAT WAS *YOUR* FAULT, BITCH! THAT SHIT IS ON *YOU!*

I DIDN'T WANT TO *SHOOT* YOUR ASS!

GODDAMN.

GODDAMN GREASE MONKEY MADE ME--

EEEE

THE HELL...?

LISTEN, I ALREADY SENT MY DAUGHTER TO SCOUT FOR THE REST OF YOUR CREW.

IF SHE COMES BACK AND TELLS US YOU LIED ABOUT *OTHER* FEDS HERE, I'M GOING TO HAVE TO TAKE THIS TO THOSE BIG BROWN *EYES* OF YOURS.

I TOLD YOU, I AM *NOT* A FEDERAL AGENT. DR. MANN AND I ARE *PHYSICIANS*, ON A HUMANITARIAN MISSION.

OH, YEAH? THEN I'M SURE YOU COULD ANSWER A QUESTION FROM MY FIRST-YEAR *NURSING EXAM.*

LIKE, LET'S SAY A PATIENT'S SUPPOSED TO GET 1000 ML OF LACTATED BRINGER'S SOLUTION IN A FIVE-SHIFT. WHAT'S THE INFUSION RATE?

...

200 MILLILITERS AN HOUR.

AND IT'S *RINGER'S* SOLUTION, NOT BRINGER'S.

SHE'S *LYING*, JOY. WHY WOULD AN M.D. BE PACKING HARDWARE LIKE *THIS?*

GIRL'S *GOTTA* BE WORKING FOR THE SCUMBAGS WHO MADE WHATEVER KILLED OUR BOYS.

THE PLAGUE *ISN'T* MANMADE. IT *CAN'T* BE. WHO WOULD *GAIN* FROM KILLING ALL THE MEN?

OH, NOT *ALL* OF THEM. I'M SURE BUSH AND CHENEY AND ASHCROFT ARE STILL ALIVE IN MOUNT WEATHER, WAITING TO RELEASE THEIR *SHOCK TROOPS* ON US.

BUT THE SONS OF ARIZONA AIN'T GONNA GO OUT LIKE THE 50,000 GIRLS RAPED IN YUGOSLAVIA, OR THE 100,000 "COMFORT WOMEN" KIDNAPPED BY THE JAPS DURING--

GOD, STOP REGURGITATING WHATEVER *PROPAGANDA* YOUR HUSBANDS FED YOU! THERE *IS* NO WAR! ALL THIS BLOCKADE OF YOURS IS DOING IS *STARVING* THE COUNTRY!

AND WE'LL CONTINUE TO STARVE IT UNTIL AMERICA'S *FEVER* BREAKS...AND THE INFECTION OF GOVERNMENT HAS *PASSED.*

UHF!

KLANG

"200 MILLILITERS AN HOUR"?

NOT BAD, 355.

WHAT, I GOT IT RIGHT?

YOU WERE BLUFFING?

EDUCATED GUESS. MY MOM USED TO BE AN RN.

SHE'D LET ME MAKE THE ROUNDS WITH HER SOMETIMES. MY TOTAL RECALL STRETCHES BACK PRETTY FAR, BUT I WASN'T SURE IF--

YOU...YOU NEVER TALK ABOUT YOUR FAMILY, 355. I DIDN'T KNOW YOUR MOTHER'S IN MEDICINE.

SHE WAS. DIED WHEN I WAS EIGHT. WITH MY DAD AND MY BABY SISTER.

CAR ACCIDENT.

I'M...I'M SORRY.

I'M SO SORRY...

I'M NOT ASKING YOU AGAIN, LADY.

WHO THE HELL ARE YOU TALKING TO?

I'M NOT A LADY.

AND I'M TALKING TO MY MONKEY.

BUT HE'S JUST A MONKEY. HE DOESN'T UNDERSTAND ME. AND THAT'S MY FAULT. I... I DIDN'T TRAIN HIM WELL ENOUGH.

HOLY FUCKING...

YOU'RE A...A...

MAN, I'M NOT EVEN *DRUNK* ANY-MORE.

I'VE NEVER *BEEN* SO SOBER. I MEAN, THIS MUST BE THE *DEFINITION* OF SOBER.

CAN I ASK HOW OLD YOU ARE?

YOU SEEM A LITTLE YOUNG TO BE A *MURDERER*.

NO...THAT CHICK DREW ON *ME*! I *HAD* TO!

SHE WASN'T A "CHICK."

HER NAME WAS P.J. SHE PLAYED THE BASS AND FIXED CARS AND--

SHUT UP, ALREADY!

YEAH, YOU SOUND LIKE MY SISTER.

SHE KILLED AN INNOCENT WOMAN, TOO.

RAAK

WE SHOULD TALK, 355.

IN A SECOND, DOCTOR. P.J. SAID THERE WERE ONLY EIGHT WOMEN IN THIS CAMP, RIGHT?

WITH JOY'S KID ON PATROL AND TWO OF HER SOLDIERS IN THE MORGUE, THAT LEAVES JUST *FIVE* PEOPLE OUT THERE. IF I CAN TIME THINGS EXACTLY RIGHT--

355, AREN'T YOU WONDERING WHY *I KEPT* LYING TO YOU ABOUT CLONING MY "SICK NEPHEW"? EVEN *AFTER* I KNEW YOU HAD NO INTENTION OF ARRESTING ME FOR MY EXPERIMENTS?

IT'S BECAUSE I DIDN'T WANT YOU TO THINK I WAS SOME KIND OF *MAD SCIENTIST.* I KNOW IT'S JUVENILE, BUT I...I WANTED YOU TO *LIKE* ME.

I *DO* LIKE YOU, ALISON.

HOLD ON.

YOU MEAN...*LIKE* YOU LIKE YOU?

JESUS, YOU'RE EVEN STARTING TO *TALK* LIKE YORICK.

I MEAN, I'VE ALWAYS KNOWN YOU WERE...*YOU KNOW,* BUT I NEVER THOUGHT YOU HAD ANY INTEREST IN--

YOU TWO STILL PLAYING DOCTOR?

133

Three Hours Later

YORICK, WHAT *HAPPENED?*

355. DOC.

ARE... ARE YOU GUYS *OKAY?*

WHAT *IS* THIS, 'RICK?

WHERE'S P.J.?

SHE WAS *ATTACKED.* BY ONE OF THE GIRLS FROM THAT MILITIA. THEY... THEY ENDED UP *SHOOTING* EACH OTHER.

I WANTED TO DO SOMETHING, BUT...BUT AMPERSAND *LOST* THE GUN YOU GAVE ME, SO ALL WE COULD DO IS HIDE.

I'M SUCH A COWARD, I--

DON'T BE RIDICULOUS, YORICK.

YOU DID THE RIGHT THING.

WHAT ABOUT YOU TWO? WHERE *WERE* YOU?

WE'LL TELL YOU ON THE WAY TO DR. MANN'S BACK-UP LAB IN SAN FRAN. I DON'T WANT TO SPEND ANOTHER SECOND OUT HERE.

BUT THE *ROADBLOCK*...

IT'S *UNBLOCKED*.

P.J. DIDN'T GIVE HER LIFE IN VAIN. MILLIONS OF PEOPLE WILL BE ABLE TO GET PROVISIONS NOW THAT I-40 IS OPEN AGAIN.

CHRIST, HOW MANY MORE WOMEN HAVE TO *DIE* BEFORE WE CAN *SAVE* THEM?

I CAN'T APOLOGIZE ENOUGH, YORICK.

THIS ALL STARTED BECAUSE I DIDN'T TELL YOU AND 355 THE *TRUTH*. BUT I PROMISE, FROM HERE ON OUT...

...NO MORE LIES.

Oldenbrook, Kansas
Now

THE ASTRONAUT WOMAN?

BUT HER CHILD TODDLER--

--CAME A FEW DAYS EARLIER THAN EXPECTED.

ONE SECOND, DR. WEBER WAS GOING INTO LABOR, AND THE NEXT, THE BABY WAS *CROWNING!* I'VE NEVER SEEN SUCH AN EFFORTLESS--

Y? Y? Y? AND? AND? AND?

AND EVERYTHING'S FINE.

HER *SON* IS FINE.

ALIVE?! A MALE WITH ACTUAL BREATH IS PASSING THROUGH THE VAGINA!

SPASIBO, IISUS HRISTOS! SLAVA BOGU!

UM. RIGHT!

BUT WE'LL HAVE TO KEEP THE BOY DOWNSTAIRS IN THE HOT SUITE UNTIL WE'RE *CERTAIN* THAT THE ENVIRONMENT POSES NO THREAT TO HIM. MY SISTER AND I THINK--

PARDON ME.